My New Best Friend

My New
Best Friend

Wendy Loggia

A Skylark Book
New York · Toronto · London · Sydney · Auckland

RL 3.5, AGES 007–010

MY NEW BEST FRIEND

A Bantam Skylark Book / June 2001

ISBN: 0-553-48735-3

Visit us on the Web! www.randomhouse.com/kids

**Educators and librarians, for a variety of teaching tools, visit us at
www.randomhouse.com/teachers**

Published simultaneously in the United States and Canada

BANTAM SKYLARK is an imprint of Random House Children's Books, a
division of Random House, Inc. SKYLARK BOOK and colophon and BANTAM
BOOKS and colophon are registered trademarks of Random House, Inc.
Bantam Books, 1540 Broadway, New York, New York 10036.

PRINTED IN THE UNITED STATES OF AMERICA

OPM   10   9   8   7   6   5   4   3   2   1

For Mom and Dad, who put up with the barking,
the dog hair, and the furry black paws
inching into the living room

Chapter One

"And this was Hamlet, my dachshund," Minnie told Kaia, pointing to the photograph in her wallet. "We had to put her to sleep when she was twelve."

Kaia Hopkins reached out to touch the plastic sleeve as her four-year-old sister, Bug, leaned over her shoulder to look.

"That's so sad," Kaia said as her babysitter carefully closed her wallet. Kaia's mom was a caterer. She worked three days a week, and when she did, Minnie came over to watch Kaia and her two sisters. "Do you think you'll get another dog?"

"I'd love to," Minnie said. "But not while I'm in college. There wouldn't be anybody home to take care of it." She shrugged. "And it made me feel so sad when we put Hamlet to sleep that I don't know if I *want* to love another dog."

Kaia sighed. "But isn't it like that old saying? It's better to have loved and lost than never to have loved at all?"

"Huh?" Her nine-year-old sister, Kristy, looked up from the book she was reading.

"You know—like, it's better to have had a dog to love than never to have had a dog at all," Kaia went on. She leaned back in her chair at the kitchen table. "Who knows if *I'll* ever get a dog to love?"

Kaia wanted a dog more than anything. She had even started a dog club called Woof! with her best friends, Emily and Lauren, and Samantha, a new girl in their class. At first Emily had been the only one with a dog. Now Lauren had one too. Kaia and Sam were still waiting.

And waiting. And waiting.

"May I have some more milk, please?" Kaia asked, holding out her empty glass.

Minnie looked puzzled. "Didn't I just fill that a minute ago?"

"She's giving it to Purr," Bug whispered.

Kaia frowned. "I can still hear you when you whisper like that, you know!" she said as Minnie ducked under the table and pulled out the small plastic bowl Kaia had been filling with milk. Purr, the Hopkins family's slim gray cat, meowed as he crept out from behind Kaia's legs.

"Listen, you guys, I need to concentrate," Kristy complained. She gestured to the piles of paper and books around her. "How am I supposed to learn about the six states of the New England region with all this racket?"

"Well, I'm working on compound words," Kaia said, pointing to her half-done paper. She should have had it finished, but she had been too busy sneaking bowls of milk to Purr—and talking.

"And I'm working on leaves for hearts and crafts," Bug said proudly, waving a green crayon.

Kaia giggled. Bug liked to pretend she went to Curly Maple Elementary School with Kaia and Kristy. She was only four, though. And she was always getting words wrong. "Do you want to help me with my compound words?" Kaia asked her. "I bet we could come up with some really funny ones!"

Before Bug could answer, Minnie took away their crumb-filled plates. "Okay, ladies," she said, "snack time is over. Your mom will be home soon, and you know she's going to check your progress."

Kaia settled back in her seat and looked

at her paper. "Which compound word is a berry that is blue?" she mumbled, twirling her pencil. "Blueberry," she said, answering her own question. She printed the word on the blank line. "Which compound word is a boat to sail? A—"

The ringing of the telephone cut off her answer.

"I'll get it!" Kaia shouted as Kristy covered her ears. She lunged for the phone on the wall.

"Hello, Hopkins residence. How may I direct your call?" she asked breathlessly.

The female voice on the other end laughed. "This has got to be Kaia."

"Aunt Beryl!" Kaia squealed. Aunt Beryl was her mom's younger sister. She lived in Philadelphia, and she was very cool. She dressed like the movie stars Kaia saw on TV, and she always smelled great. "Mom isn't home," Kaia told her. "She's making cheese blintzes at the Stuffed Mushroom."

That was the name of the catering shop where her mother worked.

"Oh," Aunt Beryl said, and Kaia realized she sounded kind of upset. "I was hoping to catch her before I ran out to my yoga class."

"Is everything okay?" Kaia asked. Her stomach did a little flip-flop.

"Not exactly, honey," Aunt Beryl said. "You remember that I'm supposed to move to New York City in two weeks, right?"

Kaia nodded. "Oops. Yes," she said, remembering her aunt couldn't see her nod. "You have to move because you got a fabulous new job with great benefits working for some magazine." That was what her mom had said, anyway.

Aunt Beryl cleared her throat. "That's right. But you see, I just found out that my new apartment building doesn't allow dogs."

"But what about Fred?" Kaia asked,

horrified. "They can't tell you you can't bring him!" Fred was Aunt Beryl's basset hound. He was just as cool as Aunt Beryl.

Kaia thought back to the moment two years ago earlier when she'd first seen Fred. Her family had gone to visit Beryl, and the basset hound had been only a few months old. Those big sad eyes, those long droopy ears . . . Kaia had fallen in love. She hadn't seen him since then, but she knew he'd still be just as cute.

"I'm afraid they can," Aunt Beryl said, sniffling. "The apartment I'm moving into is a studio."

"Like a film studio?" Kaia asked, somewhat cheered up. There would probably be all sorts of famous people there. They wouldn't even notice a little dog like Fred. . . .

"A studio is a really, really small apartment," Aunt Beryl explained. "And in this case, it's a small apartment that doesn't allow dogs."

"What meanies!" Kaia burst out.

Everyone Kaia knew liked animals. She looked anxiously over at Purr, who was arching his neck. What if someone said they had to get rid of him? Or Gertie, her sister Bug's chubby goldfish? When Kaia was in preschool, her family had owned a ferret! And Kaia's dad had had an iguana when he was in college. They were definitely a pet kind of family.

Kaia plopped with a thud onto the kitchen floor. It sure would be hard to give up a great dog like Fred. "Could you find another apartment?" she asked hopefully.

"I don't want to. This one has everything I need." Her aunt sighed. "A small apartment wouldn't be fair to a dog like Fred. And to be honest, I haven't been able to spend as much time with Fred as he deserves. He'd be better off with a new owner, but I've got to find one fast. I thought maybe your mom might know of a wonderful person who could take him."

Lightbulbs began clicking on in Kaia's brain. "I know someone who could take him!" she shouted into the phone, ignoring Kristy's glare. "Us! Give him to us!" Her family could adopt Fred! It was the perfect solution!

Her aunt was quiet for a few seconds. "Gee, I don't know, Kaia," she said. "That's a lot to ask."

"No! No, it's not," Kaia said, leaping to her feet. "We'd be perfect! Fred already knows us, and we'd love him like crazy. You could even visit him whenever you felt like it." As the words rushed out of Kaia's mouth, she grew even more excited. This could be the answer to her aunt's prayers—and hers, too!

"I have a picture of me and Fred in a construction-paper frame," Kaia rushed on. "The frame has an outline drawing of my handprint and Fred's tiny paw print!"

"Honey, Fred isn't a puppy anymore," Aunt Beryl said. "He's grown into a full-sized dog."

"Oh, I know," Kaia said, her mind racing to which friend she should call first. Fred could join the Woof! Club with her!

"Hearing your voice cheers me up so much, Kaia, and I appreciate your offer," Aunt Beryl went on, "but this is too big a decision to make on your own."

"Please let me ask Mom and Dad," Kaia begged. She looked at the kitchen clock. Her parents would be home any second. "I know they'll say yes. I just know they will!"

They had to!

"Well . . . you can mention it to them," Aunt Beryl said at last. "But I'll call back tonight and talk to your mom about all this. I'm not making any promises now, you hear me?"

"Okay, Aunt Beryl. Love you!" Kaia clicked off. She put the phone back, then placed both hands on the kitchen table. She shoved Kristy's homework and Bug's pumpkin drawings aside.

"Listen up," she told her sisters. "We've got real work to do!"

Chapter Two

"Okay, this is it. Operation Sweet Talk is going down," Kaia said under her breath, motioning for Bug and Kristy to get into place. Their mom's car had just pulled into the driveway, and Kaia had hatched a plan to make sure her parents said yes to Fred.

For once, Bug and Kristy were willing to go along with her. Of course, she'd had to promise Bug she'd read an extra story at bedtime, and Kristy had weaseled a night of drying dishes out of her. But when Kaia told her sisters what Aunt Beryl had said, she could tell they were almost as excited as she was.

"Greetings, Queen of the Castle!" Kaia said when her mom stepped inside the house. She gave her a big smooch on the cheek. "We are here to do your bidding."

Minnie picked up her car keys with the Mickey Mouse key chain. "You're in for the star treatment tonight, Mrs. H.," she said, winking as she closed the back door behind her.

"I guess I am," Mom said, looking a bit bewildered.

"Here, let me take that," Kristy said, helping her shrug out of her pea coat. She hurried to hang it up in the closet.

"Iced tea, with extra sugar and a dash of lemon juice. Just like you like it," Kaia said, holding out a cold glass.

Her mom's eyes widened. "Why, thank you."

Ooh, her plan was working! Kaia steered her mom into the living room. "Why don't you sit down?" She patted the sofa. "Doesn't this look comfortable?"

Mom raised her eyebrows as she sat down and took a sip of tea. "Mmmm. Now, this does hit the spot."

Bug came running from their parents' bedroom. She held out a pair of fuzzy pink slippers. "Are your feet tired, Mommy?"

Mrs. Hopkins laughed. "Whatever your sisters want must be big if even you're in on it."

"Where are my girls?" Mr. Hopkins's voice carried in from the kitchen.

"Daddy!" Bug said, dropping the slippers and running to greet him.

Swiftly Kaia slid the slippers onto her mom's feet.

"Why do I have a feeling you're the one behind all this?" her mom asked.

Kaia shrugged, feeling as if she were going to burst! She wanted to blurt out Aunt Beryl's exciting news right then and there. But she bit her tongue. She had to make sure she didn't waste her opportunity. Her mom and dad had to be in the best moods ever before she asked them about Fred.

"The king has arrived in his castle," Kaia said dramatically as her dad stepped into the living room. She gave a slight bow.

"Don't overdo it," Kristy muttered in her ear. She gave their dad a hug. "I'll get you some iced tea too, Dad. We made it with Minnie."

"Me and Bug'll be right back," Kaia said, grabbing her little sister's hand. "Okay," she said when they got into the hall. "Remember what I said. You get Purr. I'm going to get Gertie."

"Okay," Bug said, her face serious.

Kaia ran to Bug's room and picked up the goldfish bowl. She met up with Bug and Purr in the hall and they carried their pets into the living room.

"Don't swish her so much," Bug said worriedly as Gertie swam in frantic circles. Purr just purred.

Their dad was sitting by their mom, a glass of iced tea in his hand. Both of them looked happy—and just a teeny bit suspicious.

Perfect! Operation Sweet Talk was going exactly according to plan. Kaia gently put Gertie's bowl on the coffee table, while Bug dropped Purr onto the rocking chair, where he curled into his favorite position.

"You look very handsome tonight, Dad," Kristy said as she, Kaia, and Bug lined up in front of them.

"Mom's beauty is lighting up your life, isn't it?" Kaia said.

Mom snorted a laugh. A dribble of iced tea danced down her chin.

"I'll get that," Kaia whispered, dabbing her mom's face with a tissue.

"Okay, close your eyes," Bug instructed when Kaia was finished. Their parents exchanged glances but did as they were told.

"What is our family missing?" Kaia asked as Kristy ran over to the desk and picked up three masks.

In unison, Kaia and her sisters each put on a basset hound mask. It had been a stroke of genius, Kaia thought. They had made the masks from Bug's construction paper. There were even long brown ears! Minnie had shown them how to fasten the masks around the back of their heads with rubber bands.

"Ta-da!" Kaia let her parents laugh for a moment. Then she sprang it on them. "Aunt Beryl wants us to adopt Fred!"

"Her new apartment doesn't allow dogs," Kristy said.

"But our house does," Bug added.

"Please, please, please, with sugar and icing and sprinkles and granola and chocolate chips on top?" Kaia dropped to her knees. "Oh, please let us get Fred, Mom and Dad. Please!"

Operation Sweet Talk had turned into Operation Beg. Kaia said everything she could think of that might convince her parents to let them adopt Fred. After all, she wasn't pleading to get just any dog—she was pleading for Fred! Gentle and loving Fred.

"Whoa, girls!" Mom held up her hand to shush them. "Dad and I are going to need to speak privately about this. And I want to speak with your aunt, too."

Kaia could barely concentrate during dinner. And afterward, she could hardly stand more waiting as her parents talked things over. Then Kaia's mom phoned Aunt Beryl.

Kaia and Bug did a nervous dance in the kitchen as they listened. Kristy pretended to be making herself a sundae, but Kaia knew she was listening in too.

"Out!" Mom said after Bug stepped on her toe. They traipsed into the living room. Kaia tried to sit down on the sofa, but it was no use. She tiptoed to the corner. Bug was behind her. Kristy was behind Bug.

They eavesdropped.

"Mm-hmm," Mom was saying. "Good-natured and sociable. Hmmm. Yes. Good family dog. Moderate exercise. Weekly brushing." Mom laughed. "I can't believe we're doing this either, Beryl. But we will."

"We will?" Kaia shouted out, running into the kitchen. "Aunt Beryl's going to give Fred to us?"

Mom nodded as Kaia threw her arms around her. "Oh, thank you, Mom. Thank you so much!"

"We're going to get a doggie. We're going to get a doggie," Bug began to sing as Kristy swung her in a circle.

Kaia was itching to speak with her aunt. "Let me talk to her, please, Mom? Let me talk to her!" she pleaded until her mom gave her the phone.

"Thank you so much, Aunt Beryl!" Kaia squealed into the receiver. "I know you must feel bad having to give Fred up, but I promise we'll make him feel right at home."

As soon as she'd handed the phone back to her mom, Kaia raced to her room, her heart thumping so hard she thought it might actually pop out of her chest. Her fingers tore through the contents of her desk drawer until she found what she was looking for.

It was the photograph of her six-year-old self with Fred.

"In nine days you'll be here, Fred," Kaia whispered, clutching the photo to her pounding chest. "Here with me!"

Chapter Three

"**M**rs. Williams gave us too much homework," Emily complained, her dark hair blowing out behind her. "Homophones *and* five-digit numbers *and* reading."

Lauren let out a deep sigh. "I guess it's because we're in third grade now."

"We get a lot more homework here than in my old school in Ohio," Sam told them.

Kaia kept her purple suede shoes in sync with Lauren's rainbow-laced sneakers as the four friends walked home from school on Friday. She had her schoolbooks in her satchel, but she had a feeling she wouldn't be spending much time looking at them.

Sam shifted her small shoulders under her heavy backpack. "Aren't weekends supposed to be for fun?" she asked, squinting her hazel eyes in the afternoon sun.

"Are you kidding?" Kaia said, putting a little skip in her step. "This weekend is going to be the most fun ever. It's D-Day!"

"D-Day is dog day," Emily whispered to Sam. Sam had just moved to Lakeville a few weeks earlier. "I've known Kaia a long time. That's how I know what she means."

"Fred is so lucky to get an owner like you, Kaia," Lauren told her as they crunched through a pile of leaves. "I know you're going to make him really happy."

"He's going to make me happy too," Kaia said, picturing the moment when she would lay eyes on him once more. "I can't wait to hug him!"

"I'm so excited for you," Emily bubbled. "All our dog dreams are coming true!"

"How will you know if you do make him happy, though?" Sam asked as they looked both ways, then crossed onto Ivy Street. The crossing guard waved to them. "Basset hounds always look sad."

"I'll know," Kaia said confidently. Her dad had ordered a book about bassets from an online bookstore for her. She was going to make sure that Fred was the happiest dog on the planet!

"Why *do* bassets look so gloomy?" Lauren asked Emily. Kaia was curious about that too. And if anyone knew the answer, Emily did. She knew everything about dogs.

"Wellllll," Emily began, "maybe it's the way their eyes droop."

"Or all those wrinkles on their foreheads," Sam added.

"Wouldn't you be sad if your ears were that long?" Lauren asked with a giggle. She ran her fingers through her blond hair. "They're as long as my hair!"

Kaia frowned. A dog didn't have to have little eyes or short ears or furry hair to be loved. "I like all those things," she said firmly. "That's what makes basset hounds special."

"Did you know basset hounds were bred to hunt rabbits and other small animals?" Emily's face wore the serious expression it usually did when she talked about dogs. "Their long ears helped stir up and hold the rabbit's scent so their noses could smell it."

"Rabbits?" Lauren bit her lip. "What, um, happened when they caught the rabbit?" She shivered, pulling her sweater tighter. "Coco would never chase a rabbit. My wittle bichon frise just wikes to cuddle."

Kaia tried to imagine Fred chasing a helpless little bunny.

Sniffing.

Hunting!

Then she shook the image from her head. "Fred's not like that," she declared. "He loved cuddling with me last time."

"Lucky would be a terrible hound," Emily said. "She's one hundred percent Labrador. She just likes to roll around and nibble my toes!"

"Brighton would be awful too," Lauren said. "All he wants to chase is a Frisbee." Brighton was the Airedale terrier that Emily walked twice a week.

"Have you taken Lucky with you when you walk Brighton?" Sam asked.

Emily shook her head. "Nope, but I will soon. She's big enough now." Emily smiled. "Kaia, once you get Fred, your life is going to change forever. No more sleeping in!"

"Yeah, Kaia," Lauren said. "Get ready to work! Coco needs to be brushed and fed and walked every day." She lowered her voice. "You'll even have to clean up poopies."

"Getting a dog must be like having another person in your family," Sam said, twirling her long brown braid between her fingers.

"I guess," Kaia said slowly, not liking the idea of all that work. She knew that what Emily and Lauren were saying was true—they had dogs and she didn't. Still, her situation was different. She decided to remind them of that.

"Fred isn't a puppy," she pointed out as they approached Emily's house. "He's a full-grown dog. He's past a lot of the stuff that Coco and Lucky still need to learn." She grinned. "He's already housetrained."

"That's a good thing about getting an older dog," Emily said. "What do you think, Sam? Do you want to get a puppy or a grown-up dog?"

"I—I'm not sure," Sam answered slowly. She hunched her backpack up over her shoulders. "I guess I'll know the right dog when I see him."

"Or her," Lauren chimed in.

Kaia and her friends waved good-bye to Emily as she ran up her walkway. "See you guys tomorrow!" she called out when her mom opened the front door.

As Sam and Lauren started talking about school, Kaia imagined what it would be like to have Fred. Even if his eyes drooped and he needed to be brushed every day, she knew he was going to be just wonderful. She thought of all the fun she'd had walking Brighton and playing with Lucky and holding Coco.

Now she was going to have the chance to do everything with her very *own* pooch!

Kaia could take *Fred* for walks and chase *Fred* around the yard and hold *Fred* in her arms.

But she would definitely keep him far, far away from rabbits.

Chapter Four

"Perfect!" Kaia said as Emily tacked up a hand-painted banner on the Hopkinses' garage on Saturday afternoon. It read, FRED, YOU ROCK! The days since Kaia had found out she'd be adopting Fred had raced by, and today was the day Fred would become an official Hopkins.

Emily gave the banner an admiring look. "This neon paint with the big letters is really cool."

"I want to make sure Fred can see it right away," Kaia said. She stood there for a moment, making sure the sign wasn't crooked. Then she ran over to where Lauren was sitting cross-legged on the sidewalk.

"Aren't these cute?" Lauren asked, holding up a charcoal-colored dog bone. "I thought it would be fun to line the front walkway to your house with them!"

Kaia grinned. "That is such an awesome idea," she said.

Lauren smiled back. "I hope you don't mind that I put one in my pocket for Coco," she said, patting her jean jacket.

"Take two!" Kaia said before scampering up to the front porch. Samantha was busily blowing up balloons and tying them to the porch railing. Her cheeks were bright red.

"I never knew how hard blowing up balloons is," Sam said, putting a yellow ribbon on the end of a green balloon. "My face is tired."

"You were really nice to come and do this," Kaia said, giving Sam's shoulders a squeeze. "I know Fred will really appreciate it." She gazed at all her friends hard at work. "*I* appreciate it."

This was probably the biggest day of Kaia's life, and it meant a lot that her friends had wanted to help her make things just right.

Of course, her family was pitching in too.

"I don't think he likes this," Bug said from the other side of the porch as she tried unsuccessfully to tie a bow around Purr's neck.

"He has to wear it," Kaia said firmly. "It's for Fred."

"It's for Fred," Bug repeated sternly to the squirming Purr.

"Yo, Woof! Club!" Kristy yelled from the backyard. "Come and see what we've done!"

Kaia raced around the house, with Lauren and Emily and Sam on her heels. Kristy and her dad were putting the finishing touches on the new doghouse her dad had built especially for Fred.

"Wow!" Emily yelled.

"It will keep Fred protected," Lauren said happily.

"Nice color," Sam said, pointing to the fresh coat of red paint.

"I love it!" Kaia cried.

"Now all we need is a dog," Dad said, standing up and brushing his hands against his pants.

"Not just any dog," Kaia said, turning to her friends.

"Fred!" they all yelled.

"I think that's them!" Kaia shouted, pushing the curtain out of the way. Then she slumped back on the couch next to Emily as the car that didn't belong to Aunt Beryl passed by. "When are they going to get here?" she fretted.

"It's really hard to wait," Lauren said sympathetically. She nibbled on one of the orange-frosted cookies Kaia's mom had put out.

The clock on the mantel ticked. And tocked. The hand was moving even more slowly than the one in their school class-room.

"Maybe she got lost," Sam said, rocking back and forth in the rocking chair.

Kaia didn't think so. "No, Aunt Beryl's pretty good with directions. And she's been here before."

Could something have happened to Fred on the way to her house? What if he was afraid of being cooped up in a cage? Or got carsick? After all, it was a six-hour drive. Kaia had gotten carsick once. It had been awful. She squeezed her eyes shut, trying to think happy thoughts.

"Does your aunt drive a green SUV with Pennsylvania license plates?" Emily blurted out, rising up on her knees to stare out the window.

"Yes!" Kaia exclaimed, sitting up straight, her eyes wild.

Emily looked guilty. "Um, she's not here. I just wanted to make sure I knew what to look for."

Kaia groaned and flung her arm over her face. The anticipation was killing her!

Nobody said anything else.

Nobody even ate a cookie.

"Why are you guys sitting around like sad sacks?" Bug asked, hopping into the room and fastening her Velcro-strapped sneakers. "Don't you want to make Aunt Beryl and Fred feel welcome?" She ran out the front door.

Kaia looked at her friends, then out the window. "They're here!"

The Woof! Club raced out. Aunt Beryl's SUV was parked in the driveway, the front windows rolled down. Kaia's parents were already there, talking with her aunt.

"Fred!" Kaia called out, trying to get a look inside. There were some boxes and bags and a large metal cage. "It's me. Kaia!"

Aunt Beryl hugged her. "You're not excited or anything, are you?"

"Hurry, Aunt Beryl. I'm going to burst if I don't see him soon!" Kaia exclaimed.

Everyone stepped back as Aunt Beryl and Mr. Hopkins maneuvered the travel cage. Kaia could hear Fred sniffling and snorting.

"Fred, you're here! Your new home!" Kaia said as the grown-ups got the cage free and put it on the driveway.

A pair of big brown eyes stared back at her. And the eyes weren't all that was big. Fred's ears were huge. His snout was even huger!

Sam gasped. "He's so big!"

"I bet he can't wait to stretch his legs," Emily said.

Kaia peered at the cage. What legs? All she could see was ears and extra skin.

Lauren held her nose. "Pee-yew! What's that smell?"

The rest of the Hopkins family stared, openmouthed.

"Everybody, this is Fred," Aunt Beryl said proudly, unfastening the lock. "And don't worry, he might look large, but he's as gentle as a lamb."

Kaia crouched down so she was nose to nose with the basset hound. Could this big bowwow really be the puppy she'd fallen in love with?

"What a good boy," Emily said between coughs, petting Fred's squatty body and kissing his head.

"Look at his ears, Kaia," Lauren squealed. "Look at his ears!" They were long and brown and looked really soft.

Sam started to cough too. "He needs some doggie perfume, I think."

"Major perfume," Kristy declared from beside Bug. They were both making faces and holding their noses.

Kaia reached out and softly stroked Fred's head. So what if he was a little stinky? "We tried to make everything real nice for you," she said as he gave her a sad look. "Do you see the balloons and the banner? They're for you!"

"Sorry about the smell," Aunt Beryl apologized, running her fingers over her short hair. "Usually I give him a bath once every two months and clean his ears out every week, but with the move and all, I haven't had time."

"Leave it to us. A bath is the first item on our agenda," Kaia's mom said.

"Yipe!" Kaia cried as Fred's long, wet pink tongue licked her hand, covering it with drool.

A wave of doggie odor blew over her as she wiped her palm on her gold velour jeans and then bent down and gave Fred a hug.

Fred was smellier and larger than she could ever have imagined.

What had she gotten herself into?

Bath? Did that lady say bath?

News flash! I'm not taking one.

No way.

Nothing doing.

Uh-uh.

Who are all these small people?
They smell funny. And they cough
a lot.

One more thing. Why did my
food slave Beryl bring me here?

Fred

Chapter Five

"Fred ate like a horse tonight, didn't he?" Kaia said before taking another bite of her green beans. Aunt Beryl had filled up his dog bowl and he'd gobbled every morsel. Right now he was sitting out on the patio. They had left the light on so they could see him even though it was dark. "No, not a horse," Kaia amended. "A hippo!"

"Usually I feed him a few small meals a day instead of one big meal, but I didn't want to feed him very much this morning since we had to drive all the way here,"

Aunt Beryl said, sipping her ice water. "He eats about three cups of dry food a day. I've written everything down for you."

"Are you sure you gave him enough tonight?" Kaia asked. Fred looked so sad, she thought maybe his tummy wasn't quite full.

Aunt Beryl chuckled. "Don't make the mistake of feeding him out of pity. That will only make him fat—and his legs already have enough weight to support."

"Just how heavy is he?" Kaia's dad asked.

"About seventy pounds."

"That's more than me!" Kristy exclaimed.

"Whoa," Kaia said, thinking of how little Lucky and Coco were. "I guess he's too big for me to pick up."

"Don't even try it," her mom told her.

Kaia nodded. "Are you feeling sad about leaving Fred, Aunt Beryl?" she asked. Her aunt was sleeping over, but tomorrow, she was headed for New York City. Kaia knew she sure would be blue.

Her aunt sighed. "Yes, but my furbaby's going to be really happy here with all of you. So that makes me feel better."

"Your furbaby?" Kaia repeated, trying not to laugh.

Aunt Beryl smiled. "That's what basset owners like to call their dogs. It fits, doesn't it?"

Kaia scrunched her lips. "Well..." Fred didn't exactly look like a baby.

Her mom glanced out at the patio. "Is there anything special we should know about taking care of Fred?" she asked.

Aunt Beryl smiled. "Fred is a wonderful dog, but like any pet, he does have a few tiny shortcomings."

Kaia giggled. *Tiny* was one thing Fred was not!

"Okay, first of all, you already know

that he can be kind of smelly," Aunt Beryl began.

"We sure do," Kristy said, shuddering. "I've never smelled anything like him!"

"Did you ever smell your feet?" Kaia said, frowning. Kristy made a face. Then their mom gave them a look and they stopped.

"I bathe him every month or two, brush him regularly, and clean his ears once a week," Aunt Beryl said. "He has a special solution from the vet to get the gunk out from inside his ears, and you have to wipe the outside of them too. They're so long they get in his dog food and water and sometimes they trail on the ground!"

"I'll do everything," Kaia said excitedly. She couldn't wait to shampoo Fred's hair and brush his long velvety ears—once they were clean, that was.

"He drools a lot," Aunt Beryl went on.

"You'll need to have a rag ready. He can make a real mess, especially when he drinks." She laughed. "I hope you don't mind dog drool on your floors and walls."

"Walls?" Kaia's mom repeated, raising her eyebrows.

Aunt Beryl nodded. "Walls." She dabbed a napkin on her lips. "Speaking of walls, Fred will wander away if he's not fenced in. And never let him off his leash."

"We don't have a fence," Bug piped up.

Dad sighed. "Looks like we'll be getting one."

Aunt Beryl looked at each of them. "I know this is a big undertaking for all of you, and I can't tell you how much I appreciate it. Fred is a lot of work—but he's a real gentle soul, and he's great with kids. You're going to love him."

"We already do," Kaia said happily.

After dinner, Kaia tried to introduce

Fred to Purr. "We want to do this slowly," Mom said. "We don't want Purr to think he's been replaced."

"They have to get used to each other's scent," Kaia said as Purr ran from the room. "I guess Purr doesn't like it any more than we do!"

The rest of the night Kaia stuck to Fred like tape. She patted his head and rubbed his back and whispered all the fun things she had in store for him into his long ears. And she listened closely to all the instructions Aunt Beryl gave her.

When it was time for bed, Fred waddled down the hall behind Kaia to her room. But he wouldn't go in. He sat down in the hall. And he didn't move.

Kaia tugged gently on Fred's collar. "Come on, Fred. You get to sleep in my room!"

"It's only half your room," Kristy said from inside, pulling her nightgown over her head. "And my half doesn't want him in it until he has a bath."

"What if I want him here?" Bug asked, peeking out from her sleeping bag.

"It doesn't count. You're only in here so Aunt Beryl can have her own room," Kristy told her.

Kristy was so bossy! "You get to have Purr sleep with you, so I get to have Fred," Kaia said firmly. She gave the basset another encouraging pat. "Look, Fred." She pointed to his beanbag bed in the corner of the bedroom. "See? It's your bed!" She lowered her voice. "You could even sleep *with* me if you want."

"He won't fit on your bed!" Kristy said, eavesdropping. "I'm going to tell Mom if you let him."

Kaia blew out her breath. "I'm trying to make him comfortable, and you are not helping."

Fred sat.

Kaia waited.

Fred sat.

Kristy turned the bedroom light off.

"Now I can't see what he's doing!" Kaia complained.

"He's waiting for you to go to bed, like we are!" Kristy said.

Their mom walked down the hall. "Honey, why don't we put Fred's beanbag out here?" she suggested. "Let's let him get used to being in a new place."

Kaia didn't want to. She wanted Fred to sleep right beside her. But she knew her mom was right. So together they dragged the old beanbag bed into the hallway. Fred immediately waddled over to it and lay down.

Kaia's mom smiled. "See? Dogs are like people. They don't always do what you want. Sometimes you have to compromise."

"Good night, Fred," Kaia whispered as

her mom went to tuck her sisters in. Kaia kissed Fred's brown head. "I love you." Then she got into her own bed and fell asleep.

Kaia was right in the middle of a dream—a wonderful dream in which Fred came to school with her and played the triangle in music class in front of all her friends—when a . . . a *noise* . . . woke her up.

It sounded like a siren. A security alarm. Or a foghorn!

The scary thing was that it was right outside her bedroom door.

"What's that?" Bug whispered, scared. Kristy kept on snoring.

"I'll go check," Kaia whispered back, trying to sound brave. She slid out from under her comforter and stumbled into the hall.

Aunt Beryl was standing there, yawning, in her pajamas. Fred was sitting in his bed, his face tilted toward the moonlight that shone through the living room windows.

"Did you hear—" Kaia began. Then the sound rumbled again. . . .

"Raarrrooooo!" It was a loud, rumbling wail.

A wail that was coming from Fred!

Kaia's tired eyes grew wide.

"One more tiny shortcoming," Aunt Beryl mumbled sleepily. "Fred howls."

Raarrrooooo! I have a new food slave. Her name is Kaia. She's one of the small people I told you about.

My fuzzy beanbag with the good smells is here! Yup. I was so happy to sniff it. Kaia put it in the room she goes to at night, but that cat's in there. Her mother put my bed in the living room, but that's too far away. I'm going to drag it nearer to Kaia's room.

I like being close to her.

Fred

Chapter Six

"Now, if you change your mind for any reason," Aunt Beryl began, wiping a tear from her cheek as she gave Kaia a good-bye hug, "you know you can always—"

"Of course we won't change our minds!" Kaia said brightly, stooping to give Fred a squeeze. A whiff of Fred's scent came over her. Was it her imagination or had he gotten smellier overnight? Pee-yewsky! "Me and Fred are going to get along just super."

Aunt Beryl hugged the rest of Kaia's family, then bent down next to Fred. "I'm going to miss you, big guy," she said with a sniffle, planting a kiss on the strip of white fur between the basset hound's eyes. "But I know you're in great hands. You listen to Kaia, okay?" She patted his back, then got into her car.

Kaia wished she could pick Fred up, but he was much too heavy. She had to settle for lifting one of his stubby paws and bouncing it up and down so it looked like he was waving.

"There you go," she said, resting his big paw back on the ground. Her fingers slid between the rolls of fur-covered skin.

Everyone watched Aunt Beryl drive down the street and turn the corner. "Don't be sad, Fred," Kaia said cheerfully as her family went inside. She was a little depressed to see her aunt leave already, but the excitement of being one hundred per-cent in charge of Fred buoyed her right up. "I'll e-mail Aunt Beryl and tell her all your news."

Fred didn't look too excited, though. He looked . . . bored. At least Kaia thought he did. She clapped her hands and gave his leash a tiny tug. It was hard to see his collar under all his neck folds. "Come on, Fred. It's too windy out here today. Let's go inside."

For a second she wasn't sure he would listen to her. But he waddled obediently into the house.

Purr came slinking around the corner, rubbing his gray fur against a chair. His bright green eyes flickered at Fred.

Kaia wondered if Purr was jealous. *I would be, if I were a cat and a new pet moved in.* But Fred barely blinked a droopy eyelid.

"Beat it, Purr. We've got important things to do," Kaia said, shooing him away. She rummaged through the bag Aunt Beryl had left behind.

"Okay, Fred. This'll make you feel right at home. Here's your green squeaky frog!" She tossed the toy onto the floor.

Fred sat.

"Ummmmm, okay." Kaia rummaged some more. "Oh, this, this looks like a doozy." She pulled out what looked like a rattle made of rags. "Here, Fred! Catch!" She threw it into the air and clapped.

Thud. It landed in front of Fred. He blinked.

Kaia twirled one of her corkscrew curls around her finger. Wasn't playing with your dog supposed to be easy?

"Is this something you like?" she asked hopefully, rolling a ball toward him.

A gray streak raced by and took it.

"Purr!" Kaia shouted, slapping the floor beside her. "No fair! Fred's really going to get you for that. Right, Fred?"

Fred just drooped.

Kaia wasn't sure what to do. The pressure was on. Just then Kristy stuck her head into the room. She studied Fred for a moment. "Do you think he's okay? He's acting kind of sick."

"He is sick," Kaia said, her heart rushing out to him. "Homesick!"

Now the pressure was mounting. She would do whatever it took to make Fred happy—if she could only figure out what that was.

At noon Kaia gave him his second bowl of food and made sure his water bowl was full. It was hard to tell how much he was drinking, because his ears splashed a lot of the water out!

"Do you want to take a nap?" Kaia asked him, touching the soft white whiskers that framed his nose. He looked tired. "We've got your bed here, remember?" She didn't really want him to sleep all afternoon, but she had to keep his best interests at heart.

Nothing worked. Kaia slumped on the kitchen bench. "He hates me!" she cried.

Her mom rubbed her arm. "He doesn't hate you, pumpkin. He's just trying to get settled in. Everything here is new for him. He needs some time to adjust."

"But look at him, Mom," Kaia said under her breath, just in case Fred was listening with those big ears of his. "He seems so . . . depressed. And he must worry a lot too. Check out all the wrinkles on his forehead!"

Her mom laughed. "That's just the way basset hounds are. It doesn't mean he's sad." She chucked Fred under his chins. "Why, I think old Fred is probably a real comedian once you get to know him."

"I guess," Kaia said doubtfully. Then she had an idea. Maybe her friends could figure out what Fred's problem was.

An hour later, Kaia's doorbell rang. Lauren stood on the front step, a bottle of dog shampoo and a fluffy pink towel in her hands.

"This was such a great idea," Kaia told Lauren, pulling her inside. "I called Emily and Sam, but they couldn't make it."

"Emily's going to her grandparents' house," Lauren remembered.

Kaia nodded. "She thought the Woof! Club could meet tomorrow. Coco and Lucky have had all their vaccinations now, so they can play together. Maybe when Fred sees other dogs, he'll feel like he has some friends." She took a breath. "Something's got to work."

Kaia's mom looked surprised when

they headed into the bathroom. "Don't you think it would be better to do this in the garage?"

"The garage?" Kaia was horrified. "Mom, it's too cold in there! We want to make Fred happy, not freeze him!"

Her mom sighed. "I'll get Dad. You girls are never going to get him in the bathtub by yourselves."

Relieved, Kaia spread the bathmat on the floor, and Lauren pushed back the shower curtain.

"Should we fill the tub before Fred gets in or after?" Lauren wondered aloud.

"Before," Kaia said. "Then we can get started right away."

"Okeydokey." Lauren put the stopper in and turned the water on.

"I'll get Fred!" Kaia said, skipping from the bathroom. She found him in the kitchen with her parents.

"We were brushing some of the loose

hair off his coat," her dad said, waving a brush in the air. Fred yawned.

Kaia clapped. "Come on, Fred. We've got a surprise!" Maybe it was her imagination, but Kaia was convinced Fred picked up speed as they walked to the bathroom. She hoped Fred would think it was a good surprise.

"It's all ready!" Lauren said, gesturing to the tub.

"Okay," Mr. Hopkins said. Kaia and Lauren stood back as Kaia's parents managed to lift Fred into the tub. He made a big splash when they set him down.

"He's so short he's almost under water," Lauren said, dropping next to the tub. "His ears are floating!"

Fred stuck his snout in the water, then lifted it and snorted. "He likes it!" Kaia said happily.

"Call us when you're done," said her mom with a smile. "And try to keep the water in the tub," she said before closing the door behind her.

"Okay, Fred," Kaia said, pushing on his hindquarters. "Sit down."

But Fred wouldn't budge.

"You might get tired standing," Lauren tried sweetly. Fred's paws remained planted.

"All righty, we'll do it this way." Kaia squeezed a big dollop of doggie shampoo into her hands. "Let's start with his head first and work down."

Lauren rolled up her sleeves. "You're going to smell so good, Fred. You might even get a girlfriend!"

Fred stayed still as Kaia lathered the shampoo into his body. His short hairs felt bristly under her fingertips.

"I'll do his ears," Lauren said, gently working the suds in. "They feel heavier when they're wet."

"Shampoo the outside and we'll clean

the inside with his ear wash," Kaia said. Her aunt had left a big bottle of it.

As Lauren cooed and shampooed, Kaia reached under the basset's belly and soaped there too. Suddenly Fred shifted. His tail came down. *Splash!* His heavy front paws shot up. *Splash!*

"You're tickling him!" Lauren cried as water sprayed her face.

Kaia wiped some water from her chin. "I stopped!" The tub was a wild ocean—and Fred was causing the storm! Where had all his sudden pep come from? He wagged his tail. He shook his belly. He snorted. He splashed!

"Okay, he's clean enough. Let's rinse him!" Kaia said, turning on the faucet. Fred's head darted under the running water.

"Look! He's rinsing himself," Lauren said, dabbing her face with a towel.

"No, he's not. He's drinking!" Fred's

long tongue was lapping up the water as fast as it came out. Kaia grabbed the plastic tumbler her mom used to rinse Bug and began sloshing clean water over Fred.

Lauren plunged her arms into the tub. "I'll pull the plug. Oops! That's Fred's paw," she said, laughing. She felt around. "There." Water began going down the drain.

The bathroom door opened. "Goodness," Kaia's dad said, "wasn't Fred the one who was having a bath?"

Kaia and Lauren laughed.

"I'll get his front, you girls get his back." Kaia's dad reached into the tub.

Kaia wrapped her arms around Fred's back legs. "*Umph!* He's so heavy," she grunted as they put him down on the bathmat. He gave a great big shake. Water splattered onto the walls.

"Here's your towel," Kaia said, covering his back.

"Now he has wet doggie smell," Lauren said as they toweled him dry.

"That's a big improvement," Kaia said as she cleaned the inside of his ears with a cotton pad and the special wash. His ears weren't too yucky now, though—maybe some of the gunk had come out in the water.

"There, Fred. You're all done," Kaia said proudly, sitting back and admiring him.

Fred gave her face a lick. "You're welcome!" she said, kissing his nose. She looked at Lauren. Fred was clean and dry, but Lauren was soapy and wet! "I guess we're next!" Kaia said with a grin.

Chapter Seven

"Come on, Coco. Come on and get me!" Lauren cried, galloping toward the monkey bars. Her bichon frise ran after her, her little white paws flying over the playground. The puppy wore a red sweater that matched Lauren's.

"No, get us!" Emily said, diving into a pile of crunchy leaves. Her yellow Lab, Lucky, let out a bark and dove in beside her.

"I bet you can't get my toes," Sam called, swinging high on a swing. "I'm as high as the trees!"

Kaia watched enviously from the other side of Greenside Park. While her friends and their dogs had been zooming around that Monday afternoon, she and Fred and been *waddling* around.

Fred wanted to smell *everything*. Every bush. Every leaf. Every twig. "Is there anything you won't sniff?" Kaia asked as he ambled over to a rusted metal garbage can. "On second thought, maybe I don't want to know."

She nudged Fred with her sneaker. "Don't you want to go play with Coco and Lucky?" she asked hopefully. "I know they're not as big as you, but I think you'd have fun." Coco and Lucky sure had a lot of energy. They were running and racing, leaping and jumping.

Kaia hopped from foot to foot. She had a lot of energy too. It was hard to stand there and hold Fred's leash. She wanted to move!

"Watch this, you guys," Lauren shouted. She and Coco were at the top of the biggest slide in the park.

"Be careful!" Sam called, shielding her eyes from the sunlight.

"Wheeeee!" Lauren whooshed down in a red blur with Coco on her lap. Coco's ears blew out behind her, and when they got to the bottom, she tried to scramble back up the metal slide.

"I'm going to try that with Lucky," Emily said, scooping up her dog and running over.

Kaia turned to Fred. "What do you say you and me hit the slide, pal?" she asked wistfully. Just as she'd expected, Fred ignored her and kept sniffing. Kaia sighed. Who was she kidding? Even if he'd been willing, she couldn't have gotten Fred on the slide. She couldn't even have lifted him onto the first rung of the ladder.

"Let's everybody go down together,"

Emily called out excitedly. She tucked squirming Lucky firmly under her arm and began to climb the ladder. Lauren and Coco scooted behind them. Sam was last.

"Are you coming, Kaia?" Lauren yelled down from the platform at the top.

Kaia gestured to Fred and held up her palms. Couldn't her friends see how hopeless he was? "No, you guys slide without us."

Kaia stared at Fred's leash. Aunt Beryl had told her not to take it off when they were outside, but Kaia was tired of standing around watching Fred smell things. Besides, there was no way Fred was going to go anywhere. Right?

Kaia heard her friends laughing like crazy.

Right!

"I'm going to leave you right here," she said under her breath, wrapping her end of the leash around the trunk of a birch tree. "You stay here while I go over there and play." She pointed to the swings and patted his head. "Okay?"

Fred licked her hand with his long drool-covered tongue.

"Oh, Fred, I do love you," Kaia blurted out, giving him a hug. "I know you can't help it if you're kind of—kind of poky." With a backward glance, she took off toward her friends.

"Let's do the slide thing again," Kaia told them, grinning. She looked back at Fred. As expected, he was smelling the same leaf he'd been smelling a minute before. She should have done this an hour ago!

"Is it okay to leave Fred like that?" Lauren asked, peering over at him.

Kaia nodded. "He won't even notice I'm gone."

Everyone climbed up the ladder. Emily

was first again. Kaia slid her legs around Lauren's, and Sam wrapped her arms around Kaia's stomach. "No hands!" Kaia cried as they pushed off. They were halfway down when Sam shrieked.

"No Fred!" Sam yelled, pointing over to the bushes where Kaia had left him.

Kaia's heart began to race. "Where is he?" she screamed, her eyes racing across the playground. It felt like hours before she heard Emily gasp.

"Over there!" Emily pointed toward one of the bike paths. Kaia caught a glimpse of two short stocky paws and an upswung tail heading down the trail. A leash dragged behind him.

Fred—her Fred—was running? "Move, move, move!" Kaia cried, pushing on Lauren's back. As soon as they reached the bottom, Kaia scrambled to her feet.

"Fred! Come back!" she cried, running

toward the trail. Her friends were right beside her.

"I can't believe he took off like that," Lauren panted as they entered the woods. Coco bopped up and down in her arms.

"I can," Emily said, brushing her hair from her face. Lucky ran beside them, nipping at their heels. "Don't you remember what I told you? Fred's a hunting dog, dodos!"

Sam pushed a thorny branch out of the way. "He must have picked up a good scent."

Lauren gasped. "What if he picked up a rabbit?" Then she shot Kaia a smile. "Don't worry, Kaia. We'll find him."

Kaia couldn't shoot a smile back. Instead, she blinked away tears as they ran down the bike path. She'd only had Fred for a few days, and already she'd goofed up. *I never should have left him alone—all to go on some dumb old slide,* she thought, her stomach aching. Aunt Beryl had warned her about taking Fred off the leash—but she hadn't listened.

What if Fred got hurt?

How could she ever forgive herself?

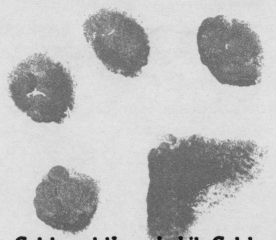

Got to get the rab-bit. Got to get
the rab-bit. Got to get the rab-bit.

Fred

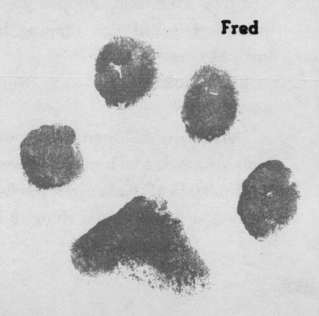

Chapter Eight

"There he is!" Sam cried as the girls and puppies burst through the woods into a clearing. Fred had stopped to sniff the ground. His tail was flipping back and forth like crazy.

Kaia choked back a sob. Her furbaby was okay!

"Raarrrooooo!" Fred let out one of his foghorn howls and lumbered forward.

"Not so fast!" Kaia threw herself at him, landing at his feet. She clung to his body.

"Don't move!" As fast as she could, she grabbed the leash.

Now that she was at Fred's eye level, she spotted a small brown bunny in the woods. "You *are* a hound dog, Fred!" she exclaimed. The bunny hesitated, then jumped away.

"We found him!" Lauren cried as Coco let out a happy bark.

"Just in time," Sam said, pointing in the direction the bunny had hopped.

"That's what hounds do," Emily reminded them. "Fred smelled something good, and his nose went after it."

"I'm just glad he didn't catch it," Lauren said, smoothing her hair behind her ears.

"You can say that again," Kaia said, kissing her dog's head a million times. She would never, ever repeat her mistake.

Lucky ran over and looked at Fred. Fred sniffed Lucky.

"I think Lucky is scared," Lauren whispered. "She's not moving!"

"Fred does look kind of scary," Sam whispered. "He's so big!"

All of a sudden, Fred gave Lucky a long wet lick.

"He kissed her!" Emily said as Lucky tried to shake off Fred's slobber.

"He liked what he smelled," Lauren said, patting his back. "Let's go swing." She placed Coco on the ground. The girls watched as the dogs trotted back down the path on their leashes.

Chasing the rabbit had given Fred a much-needed burst of energy. Kaia watched, amazed, as he sniffed Coco and Lucky.

"He's even letting them jump on his back!" Sam said as Coco climbed up on Fred—and promptly fell off the other side.

"He's a nice dog," Emily said as they came out into the park. "They're bugging him and he doesn't even care."

"He's a softie," Lauren said. She ran over and sat down on a swing while Coco scampered at her feet.

"So you think Fred smelled that rabbit?" Kaia asked as she sat down on the swing beside Lauren's. Fred sat too.

Emily nodded. "Can I peek at his dewlap?"

Kaia made a funny face. "His dew-what?"

Emily crouched down. "This." She poked at the two big folds of baggy skin under Fred's chin. "This is Fred's dewlap," she said, petting the skin. "His ears stir up good smells on the ground, his nose sniffs them, and his dewlap traps and holds the smell."

Sam perched on the zebra rocker in front of the swings. "Can you imagine Coco and Lucky with dewlaps?"

Everyone giggled at that.

Kaia was just thinking how funny Coco

would look with Fred's chin when Lucky gave the bichon's paw a nip.

Yelping, Coco scurried backward.

"Lucky, no!" Emily pulled the yellow Lab away. "She didn't mean to hurt her," she told Lauren.

Lauren stopped swinging and rubbed Coco's injured paw. "I know. They're just being puppies."

"Maybe we should keep them apart for a minute," Emily suggested. "Would you hold Lucky while I get a drink?" she asked Sam.

"Uh, sure," Sam said. Emily deposited the squirming puppy in her friend's lap and raced off to the fountain. Lauren picked up Coco and began plucking dried leaves from her sweater.

"Lucky likes this," Sam said as she rocked carefully back and forth on the zebra.

"Coco likes swinging," Lauren said as she pumped her legs high.

To Kaia's surprise, Fred jumped so his front paws were on her legs. "Do you want to swing too?" she asked, wishing more than anything that she could lift him onto her lap.

"There's no way he can swing with you," Emily declared, running back. "Bassets are not lapdogs."

"Try telling that to Fred," Lauren said gleefully as Fred attempted another jump.

"No jumping." Kaia put his stocky paws back on the ground. Aunt Beryl had told her to watch out for that, too, and she was going to follow orders this time.

"Only two more days left until Halloween," Sam said. "What are you guys wearing?"

"I'm going to be a hippie chick," Emily said. "And Lucky's going to be a hippie dog. We got her special tinted glasses."

Kaia started to feel a little anxious. It had taken her weeks to decide on her costume. Now it sounded like she was expected to have one for Fred too. And in only two days!

"My mom made me a Dorothy costume and we got a special basket to put Coco in," Lauren said excitedly. "She'll be my Toto!"

"I'm going to be a witch," Sam told them. "I'll have a green face and a big wart on my chin."

"That'll be scary," Lauren said, her eyes wide. "What about you, Kaia?"

Kaia pretended to throw a lasso. "Just call me cowgirl, cowpoke."

Emily twisted her swing around, then began to spin loose. "What's Fred going to be?"

"I'm not exactly sure," Kaia said, stumped. "I didn't know I had to dress him up."

"Oh, but you've got to!" Lauren insisted. "I can't wait to see him in a costume!"

Emily took Lucky back, and Lauren nuzzled Coco. Kaia was sure Lucky would be the cutest hippie dog ever, and Coco would make the perfect Toto.

Then she looked down at Fred, sitting peacefully at her feet. Big, droopy, short-legged Fred.

Fred was not the kind of dog that could be a hippie.

Or a Toto.

What could Fred and his dewlap possibly be?

Woof! Woof!

Woof! When I first saw Fred, I wasn't sure about him. He's big! But once I checked him out, I could tell he was a good guy. He gave me a great big lick! Emily said it was a KISS.

(Don't tell Fred, but I like Emily's kisses better.)

I didn't mean to hurt Coco. I told her I was sorry. I hope she forgives me.

Girls rule! (Emily says that a lot.)

Woof!

Lucky

Chapter Nine

"You mean he has to eat the same thing every day?" Kaia asked the next morning as her mom filled up Fred's dish with dog food. That sounded like an awful idea. What if he didn't like it? That would be like eating veal or Brussels sprouts night after night after night.

Fred sat patiently by the stove as Mrs. Hopkins put the scoop back in the bag and sealed it. "Eating the same food will make it that much simpler for you girls to remember what to feed him."

Kaia didn't mind having to feed Fred. She just wanted to make sure she knew exactly what to do.

"He must like it," Kristy said, tying her shoelaces. "It's the same stuff Aunt Beryl fed him."

Fred waddled over to his bowl and began to eat. Kaia and Bug watched as they pulled on their jackets. They had to leave for school in a few minutes.

"I've made a chore chart and put it on the fridge," Mrs. Hopkins said, pointing. "Fred's going to be counting on you to feed him and walk him and make sure his water is fresh."

"Why do we keep giving him water if he's just going to dribble it out?" Bug asked, tugging on her coat sleeve.

"Bassets are big droolers," Mrs. Hopkins said with a deep sigh. "I put an old cloth on the railing beside the trash can. That'll be Fred's slobber rag."

"You mean we have to wipe up *that*?" Kristy asked, pointing to a glistening circle of drool on the wood floor. She inched away.

Mrs. Hopkins opened the trash can cabinet, pulled out a blue rag, and tossed it to Kristy. "Yep."

Kaia was worried about something else. "I'm not sure you gave him enough to eat, Mom," she said as Fred chomped down the last dry nugget. "Doesn't he look sad and hungry?"

Her mom shook her head. "Overfeeding basset hounds is a big problem—remember what Aunt Beryl said? People feel sorry for them and give them extra food, which makes them gain too much weight." She tapped the chore chart. "Don't worry. We're following Beryl's instructions: one cup of dry food in the morning, two cups at night, and an occasional canned food supplement."

"Yuck!" Kristy held the wet rag between her thumb and pointer finger. "This is nasty!"

Kaia grabbed it, hoping Fred wasn't paying attention. "I'll clean up Fred's drool myself," she said firmly. "It's no big deal."

Kristy marched over to the kitchen sink and washed her hands. "He's all yours."

Fred stuck his head into his water bowl. He got loud and snorty when he drank, like a pig eating slops in a trough. Water sloshed onto the floor and droplets slid down his long ears.

When he'd finished slurping, he gazed up at them. A puddle of drool formed at his feet. Bug giggled.

Kristy grabbed her brown-bag lunch from the kitchen counter and tugged one of Kaia's curls. "Start mopping, squirt!"

Mrs. Hopkins gave Kristy her look that meant business. "Kristy, Fred is a part of our family and isn't just Kaia's project. We all need to pitch in. Whoever sees drool should clean it up, understood?"

Kaia began to wipe the floor. Just a few weeks before, she had told Emily that picking up dog poop was gross. She still thought it was gross, but now that she had Fred, she realized that sometimes when you had a dog, you had to do things you didn't really want to do.

But there were just so many things about Fred that she hadn't anticipated. He was big, for one. Lots, lots bigger than when she'd seen him last time. He'd quadrupled in size! She couldn't lift him onto her lap. And there was that awful foghorn bark. And the way he ran after a good smell and ignored her commands. Plus, he drooled!

Kaia had to face it—Fred just wasn't the kind of dog she'd imagined.

But now he was hers. Kaia studied the chore chart as she wiped drool. Owning

Fred was really going to keep her busy. Feeding and brushing and walking and wiping . . .

The more she thought about it, the more she felt that Fred didn't belong to her. She belonged to him!

"Have I bitten off more than I can chew?" she asked him as she hung up the rag and gave him a good-bye hug. Soft wet ears rubbed her cheeks.

I wanted a dog more than anything, Kaia thought as Fred buried his nose in her stomach. *So does it matter that you aren't quite the doggie I had in mind?*

"I did one of Coco and me and I thought you'd like one of you and Fred," Lauren told Kaia, passing the sheet of construction paper across the wide art table. Lauren had drawn a picture of Kaia and Fred together. Kaia was kissing Fred's ear, which was long enough to reach the floor.

"I love it," Kaia said loyally. Lauren was better at math than art, but she'd done a pretty good job. She'd made them both look really happy. That made Kaia feel really guilty. How could she feel anything *but* happy to have Fred? How could she sit around and wonder if another dog might have made her happier?

She was still feeling bad when construction paper got passed around.

"Today we'll be working with pastels," Mr. Kellogg, the art teacher, said, handing out boxes with what looked like squared-off chalk sticks. "Mrs. Williams tells me you're going to start a new theme next month called 'The Wonders of the Sea.'"

He hopped up to sit on a front table. "I'd like you to use your imagination and create your own wonders of the sea. What kind of sea creatures can you come up with?" He waved his paint-covered hands around in the air. "Where do they live? What do they look like? What other creatures do they see in the water?"

Everyone scrambled to get a pastel. Kaia didn't move fast enough and ended up with brown. What kind of sea creature was brown? She wanted to draw one of those fish she'd seen in the Bahamas, but they were blue and red and yellow—not brown.

"Create! Express yourselves!" Mr. Kellogg said, roaming the room.

Everyone at Kaia's table laughed. Their teacher could act kind of goofy sometimes.

Kaia frowned. Art was one of her favorite classes, but she didn't feel like drawing something from the sea. She let her fingers doodle, and before she knew what was happening, there was a sad-faced brown basset hound staring up at her.

Oh, Fred, she thought, dotting his snout with freckles. *What are you going to wear for Halloween?*

She found an orange pastel and drew a circle around him. Could he be a pumpkin? She wasn't sure where she could get a pumpkin costume for someone with Fred's measurements.

So Kaia drew some squiggly lines coming from Fred's head. Maybe she could make him a funny hat, like a jester's! She looked to see who had the purple pastel.

Just then Lauren's eyes got wide, and Kaia tried to turn over her paper before it was too late.

Too late. A shadow fell over her. "I've never seen a sea creature like this before," Mr. Kellogg said, peering at her drawing. "It might look a little strange next to the other drawings in the student work display in the hall, hmmm?"

Kaia blushed. "Sorry, Mr. Kellogg."

The art teacher smiled. "Keep creating—just don't keep your head stuck in the clouds." He picked up a green pastel and quickly drew some grass around Fred's paws before moving on.

Clouds . . . clouds . . . that was it! Kaia found a new piece of paper and started drawing the biggest brown sea horse ever. Suddenly she was inspired.

Suddenly she knew exactly what Fred's costume would be!

Chapter Ten

"Bye, Mom!" Kaia shouted over her shoulder, running to answer the doorbell. She took one last look in the mirror. Her curls danced out from underneath her cowboy hat. The brown vest with the silver trim fit over her flannel shirt just right, and the chaps on her legs made her feel like she was in the Wild West! But the best part of her costume was the lasso.

She opened the door and spun the rope in a circle. "Howdy, cowpoke."

"Ooh, you look good!" Lauren said,

clicking her glittery red heels together. Her long blond hair was in two red-ribboned braids, and she wore a white sweater over her blouse and pale blue dress. "Doesn't Kaia look good, Toto?" she asked, holding up a wicker basket. Coco sat inside, dressed in a black sweater.

"This is nothing. Wait until you see Fred!" Kaia exclaimed as the basset hound came up beside her. A halo was perched on his head, and a red bandanna was tied under his chin.

"He's a cow-angel," Kaia said proudly, clipping on his leash. "Half angel, half cowboy. The bandanna will catch his drool!"

Lauren skipped outside as Kaia shut the door behind her, and they started down Ivy Street, toward the corner where they were meeting Emily and Sam. "How did you get the halo on his head?"

Kaia put her finger to her lips. "Shhh! I

think he forgot it's there. I gave him some butter. He loves it!" One night Bug had dropped a hunk of butter on the floor and Fred had gobbled it right up. Now it was Kaia's secret weapon. "He was so busy licking his bowl, he didn't pay attention to what my hands were doing!"

Kids in costumes were racing across lawns and ringing doorbells. Some were with grown-ups, some just with other kids. Kaia was glad her parents had let her go with her friends. Trick-or-treating in Lakeville was from three until six, so it was still light out.

She spotted a witch with a long black cape and a pointy hat standing next to a girl in purple pants, a flowered shirt, beads, and a floppy velvet hat.

"Happy Halloween!" Kaia and Lauren shouted, racing forward with their dogs.

Sam let out a witchlike cackle. Emily held up her fingers in a *V.* "Peace, dudes."

"You guys look great," Lauren said as Lucky tried to jump up and sniff Coco. "I love your makeup!"

Sam's face was the color of green Jell-O. Emily had flowers painted on her cheeks.

"You look great too," Emily said as Kaia squatted down to Lucky's level.

"Where are your glasses?" Kaia asked the yellow Lab.

Emily held them up. "Lucky kept trying to bite them," she explained with an exasperated sigh.

"Fred's a cow-angel, right?" Sam asked. Her teeth were painted black.

Kaia was happy her friend had figured it out. "He didn't fit into the devil's outfit," she joked.

A group of preschool-age fairies and their moms walked by. They looked a little frightened of Sam.

"Come on, guys," Lauren said eagerly,

tugging on Kaia's arm. "Let's start tricking!"

Emily jiggled her already half-full candy bag. "I went out with my mom and Justin for a half hour." Justin was Emily's big brother. "There's a lot of candy out here!"

"One of the houses on Holly Avenue gives out full-sized candy bars," Kaia said, trying to remember which one it was from the year before.

Sam pointed down the block. "Look at all the kids down there. That's a good sign, isn't it?"

The four friends and three dogs started off.

"What do you suppose the dogs think about all this?" Sam asked as a skeleton and slice of pepperoni pizza skipped by.

"Coco—I mean Toto—is scared," Lauren admitted, holding up the basket. "See how she's crawled under the blanket?"

"Lucky doesn't like all the loud noise," Emily said as her dog scampered alongside her. "She ran and hid under my bed and wouldn't come out when the doorbell rang with trick-or-treaters."

Kaia shrugged. "Fred doesn't mind at all," she said, glancing down at him. He was waddling along beside her, his tail pointed toward the sky. His bandanna had started to get a little wet, but other than that, he looked good.

"Trick or treat!" the girls chimed at the first house they went to. A nice woman who looked like a grandma gave them all boxes of raisins.

"I hate it when people try to be healthy," Kaia said when they were back on the sidewalk.

"I know," said Emily. "It's Halloween!"

The treats at the house next door were better—lollipops and neon candies that fizzed. And at the following house, the man who answered let them choose from a big bowl. Kaia and Sam took candy bars. Emily picked a bag of chips. Lauren couldn't decide.

"Everything looks so good," she said, her fingers hovering over the candy. At last she picked a bag of chips.

The man tossed a candy bar in her sack too. "There's no reason you can't have two. Happy Halloween!"

"Why, thanks!" Lauren said happily as they stepped off the porch. "People are so nice on Halloween!"

Fred had to stop for a sniff and a tinkle. "We'll wait for you over there," Kaia told Fred, letting him run out to the end of his new retractable leash. It was really long. "He has trouble going when too many people are around," she said in a low voice as she and her friends waited on the sidewalk.

"Is he almost done?" Sam asked a few seconds later. Kaia followed her nervous gaze. A group of older, bigger boys was coming toward them. One was dressed like a vampire, one was a werewolf, and one was some kind of scary monster with crusted blood on his face. They were carrying pillowcases.

"Blaghhhh!" the monster shouted at two smaller boys dressed as dinosaurs.

"Smell my feet!" the werewolf howled, hopping on one furry leg.

The dinosaurs looked scared as they scuttled past.

"They don't look too nice," Emily whispered as Lucky let out a tiny bark.

"Let's cross the street," Lauren said under her breath, pulling her basket with Coco close to her chest.

Kaia thought that was a good idea, but Fred was still busy and there was a car coming. By the time the car had passed, the boys were right in front of them.

"Boo!" said the monster, flapping his blood-spattered arms. Even though Kaia knew it was fake blood, she shivered.

"Hey, look, Dorothy's lost the Tin Man," said the vampire as he and the boys circled them. "She's found a cowgirl, a witch, and a flapper!"

"I'm not a flapper, I'm a hippie," Emily said indignantly. She put her hands on her hips. "Get your decades straight!"

Even though Emily was right, Kaia thought maybe she shouldn't have said that. Who knew what these mean boys would do?

"Got any good candy?" the werewolf asked Sam, reaching for her bag.

Kaia was sure that if Sam hadn't been green, she'd have been white as a ghost. "No, not really," Sam squeaked.

Lucky cowered next to Emily's purple pant leg.

"We had to ring a lot of doorbells for this candy, you know," Kaia said, hoping she sounded courageous.

Ignoring her, the monster gave Lauren's braid a yank. "Our pillowcases can hold a lot more than your bags can. We'll help you carry it."

Kaia clutched her hands tightly around the leash's handle. She hated bullies.

"You better watch out or our dogs will bite you!" Lauren threatened as Coco dove under her blanket.

"Oooh, we're scared," the vampire said, chattering his fake fangs.

"Some watchdogs those fluff puffs are," sneered the werewolf.

All of a sudden a loud, rumbling growl let loose.

"What was that?" shrieked the vampire, spinning around.

Kaia gasped. There, in the shadow of the house, stood Fred. His smooth short hairs stood on end, and the tops of his long ears were raised. His halo cast a long, weird shadow in front of him.

"What is that?" the monster asked, backing up.

"*That's* our watchdog," Emily said, gloating.

"*Rrraaaarrr!*" Fred snarled. His droopy eyes were alert and trained on the bullies.

Kaia tilted her hat over her face. "And if you yellowbellies know what's good for you, you'll git out of town before sundown."

Growling, Fred took a step forward.

The bullies looked at each other—then backed away.

"We were just fooling around," mumbled the monster, shrugging under his shredded black cape.

"Yeah," said the vampire, his own teeth chattering for real this time. He smoothed back his greasy hair.

"Well, you weren't very funny," Lauren scolded, shaking her finger at them.

As Fred let out another growl, the bullies raced off.

"You saved us, Fred!" Kaia hurried over and threw her arms around him, pressing her face into his soft warm fur. Sure, Coco and Lucky were cute and fluffy, but they hadn't been able to do a thing in their time of crisis. It was Fred who had saved the day.

And their candy!

"I guess it's a Happy Howl-o-ween after all," Emily said as she and Lauren and Sam hugged and petted Fred too. Even Coco and Lucky gave him a few grateful licks.

"You can say that again," Kaia said as she squeezed her basset hound tight.

"Raarrrooooo!"

I can smell anything a mile away. And today I smelled trouble. If anyone tried to hurt Kaia or her friends, you'd better believe I'd hurt them first. Pul-ver-ize. Like Sheeba, my wise old chow chow neighbor, taught me.

Kaia's my new best friend.

Yawn.

One thing, though. I sure wish she'd take this towel off me. How am I supposed to make the floor wet wearing this?

Fred

Chapter Eleven

"That was so great when Fred let out that howl," Emily repeated, helping herself to another warm doughnut. Now that Kaia's mom had checked their bags of goodies to make sure everything was safe, the Woof! Club was in the middle of a Halloween candy trade on the Hopkinses' living room floor.

Kaia took a big gulp of her apple cider. "He was awesome. Right, Freddie?" She reached behind her circle of friends to scratch Fred's soft stomach. Coco's sweater was in Lauren's bag, and Lucky's glasses had broken, but Fred was still wearing his drool-coated bandanna. Kaia gently untied it and spread the cloth out to dry.

"Those boys were the fluff puffs, not Coco and Lucky," Lauren declared. "Hey! Trade you a Nutty Nougat for that candy corn, Sam."

"Deal." Sam tossed her the bag. "This was the best Halloween ever! Your mom is a really good doughnut maker, Kaia."

"Thanks."

Ding-dong! Coco began running in circles as Lucky rose from Emily's lap and barked.

Emily groaned. "Here we go again!"

"Don't let them see," Lauren squealed, trying to cover the dogs' eyes. "Those costumes scare them."

By now most of the trick-or-treaters had gone home. Only the older kids were still out.

"Lots of boos and barking tonight," Mr. Hopkins said with a smile as he passed by on his way to the door. "You girls have some loot there. Don't eat too much."

Lucky and Coco went crazy every time the doorbell rang, but Fred stayed calm. He'd sniffed the candy for a few minutes, then curled up behind Kaia to rest. Kaia's heart did a little *thump-thump* when she thought of how brave her basset hound had been. He had been ready to face incredible danger to protect her!

Once the door was shut, Coco settled back down in her basket and Lucky curled up on Emily's lap. Her small pink tongue licked the powdered sugar from Emily's fingers. In minutes the puppies were asleep.

Everyone got back to business.

"I've got an idea," Lauren blurted out. "Maybe the Woof! Club should have a bravery award. You know, for the dog who puts others' interests ahead of his own."

Kaia sucked in her breath. There was only one dog here who qualified for that.

"I nominate Fred!" Emily said, waving a licorice stick. "Without him, our candy would be in the hands of our enemies."

"Or in their stomachs," Sam added, nibbling her doughnut.

"All those in favor of giving Fred the award, say 'Woof!' " Lauren said.

"Woof!" they all shouted.

"Now we'll just have to figure out what the award is going to be," Lauren said with a giggle.

Kaia was sure she'd never felt happier in all her life. What made Fred different—his howl, his shape, his loyalty—was exactly what made him such a great dog.

Coco and Lucky were wonderful, but

there was no way they could have done what Fred had done today.

Fred was a hero.

Kaia yawned, snuggling closer to her basset hound. It didn't matter that he was too big to lie on their sofa. It was just as comfortable lying on the floor next to him. Fred was so big and warm, it was like having a life-sized heating pad.

Fred's breathing was slow and steady, and it seemed to Kaia that her heart beat at the same pace. She burrowed even closer. She was trying to stay awake to watch the scary cartoon that Kristy and her dad had found on TV, but somehow her eyes felt too heavy and droopy.

Her mom was on the phone in the kitchen, and her voice drifted in. "He's a perfect addition to our household, Beryl . . ."

"You are, Fred," Kaia whispered sleepily into the soft brown folds of her furbaby's ears. "You're the winner of the first Woof! award for bravery." Her arm covered his short strong paw. "And you're my new best friend."

BRUSHING, CLIPPING, AND MAKING YOUR DOG FEEL GREAT!

Keeping your dog looking—and smelling—good will make both of you feel great! Just like you need to take a bath, trim your nails, and brush your hair, dogs do too. But while you may know this, your dog may not. Some dogs may try to get clean by rolling in a pile of leaves. Others try licking themselves. That usually doesn't get them clean enough for humans. It's up to you and your family to make sure your dog is groomed regularly.

Here are a few things you'll need to learn how to do to keep your dog looking and smelling good.

Tools

You'll want to make sure you have the right grooming tools for your specific breed of dog. A steel comb, a combination bristle/pin brush, and a sturdy pair of scissors for trimming nails are all good investments. Always be gentle and loving when you use them.

Brushing

How many times a day do you brush your hair? Once? Twice? Well, if you were a Doberman pinscher, you'd only need to be brushed once a week! If you were a Shih Tzu, you'd need daily combing and brushing to make sure your long soft coat stayed tangle-free.

Brushing helps get rid of loose dirt and hair in a dog's coat. It also spreads skin oils and makes the coat shiny. When you brush your dog, you're preventing his hair from getting matted and collecting dead hair that he will eventually shed. Be gentle—just like people, dogs don't like to have their hair pulled! If you find a mat in your dog's coat, try to untangle it with your fingers, and brush or comb gently. If this doesn't work, you may have to cut it out. Be careful not to cut your dog's skin. Ouch!

Some dogs, such as poodles, don't shed. But they need to be brushed regularly so they don't develop mats. Dogs also need haircuts. Depending on the level of grooming necessary, your family might decide to do the job—or to take your dog to a professional groomer, especially if your dog has a fancy clip, as a poodle might, or a particularly long coat, such as a Maltese has. A good dog book will tell you how much brushing your breed needs.

Grooming Checklist

🐾 Clean eye discharge with a cotton pad moistened with water.

🐾 Clean earwax or discharge with a cotton pad moistened with mineral oil.

🐾 Clean teeth with a soft cloth or toothbrush. It's okay to use toothpaste, but make sure it's made for dogs.

🐾 Trim nails every few weeks. A dog's nails are shaped like crescent moons. Inside is the pink nailbed, called the quick. If your dog has white nails, you can see the quick inside; if he has black, you can't.

Never cut into the quick. The nail's nerves and blood supply are there. Cutting the quick will hurt your dog—and make him bleed. Cut off only the tip of the nail.

Bath Time

This can be a real challenge! Although dogs don't need to be bathed often—once every other month or so, depending on the breed—they do need to be shampooed so their coats stay clean and healthy.

The bathtub is probably the easiest place to bathe your dog. Use a rubber mat so your dog won't slip. Small dogs, like Chihuahuas, can even be bathed in the kitchen sink. If the weather permits, giving your dog a bath outside, using a washtub and hose, can be lots of fun!

Use warm water and a dog shampoo when you give your dog a bath. Lather your dog from head to toe. Keep the suds out of his eyes and rinse him well. He'll probably want to shake the excess water off. That's good! That means he won't be so wet. You can use a large towel to dry him. A blow-dryer can get a small dog dry very quickly!

For those times when you can't bathe your dog, brush his hair with a dry shampoo.

Grooming your dog can be one of the best things the two of you do together. Making it fun for him will make it fun for you. If you like, give your dog a special treat to eat or his favorite toy to play with when you're done.

It will be time to groom him again before you know it!

About the Author

Although she does not presently have a dog. Wendy Loggia has always loved them. Growing up, she was the proud owner of Rebel, a Siberian husky/German shepherd mix; Muffins, a toy poodle; and Nuisance, an adorable mutt who was part of her family for fifteen years. She's looking forward to the day when a furry-legged friend curls up at her feet again!

Don't miss the next **WOOF!** book

NO DOGS EVER

coming in October